Old Girls and Palm Trees

Meg Pokrass

Illustrated by Cooper Renner

BAMBOO
DART
PRESS

LOS ANGELES † NEW YORK † LONDON † MELBOURNE

Old Girls and Palm Trees by Meg Pokrass

978-1-962316-11-8   Paperback

978-1-962316-12-5   Ebook

Copyright © 2025 Meg Pokrass. All rights reserved.

First Printing 2025

Illustrated by Cooper Renner

Cover art by Dennis Callaci and Meg Pokrass

Layout and design by Mark Givens

For information:

Bamboo Dart Press

chapbooks@bamboodartpress.com

Bamboo Dart Press 055

www.pelekinesis.com

www.bamboodartpress.com

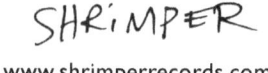

www.shrimperrecords.com

For old girls everywhere.
And for G.W.

"We have art so that we shall not die of reality"
Friedrich Nietzsche

"Now every day is easy 'cause of you…"
Crosby, Stills, Nash & Young

Contents

Visit

She is coming to visit me after all these years, says she wants to see British palm trees. It is her way of making me laugh, reminding me of a particular kind of laughter. I am so far from California palm trees now that I may as well have changed my name. *Do you have a British name?* she asks, or maybe it's me asking myself.

Remembering driving the Pacific Coast Highway all night, rolling north together, talking about nothing and everything, of making a home out of nothing. Windshield wipers sticking. The burnt smell from the bottom of the pot coffee at Perkos.

Men and palm trees, I want to say, *they kept sneaking into my life, good thing none of them caught me.*

"I don't care if you never get here," I say, low, to my lost friend, as if I'm being heard.

I don't tell her that I am leaning, that our connection has died, that I have no idea where she lives or if she is still breathing.

I am dreaming about seeing her old.

Familiar footsteps

Walking to the store for milk, I heard familiar footsteps behind me, a friend who had become a shadow that needed to be sewn back on. I stopped to listen, but the footsteps kept going, then passed. Here in the middle of an ordinary day, when no amount of movement had warmed me up. Trying not to dream about a life with the sun on my face.

Wet, Tuesday Afternoon

Today I am silent with my old friend. It is more interesting than being silent with myself. I have flopped down in our bungalow on a fine, wet Tuesday afternoon. She looks inside the doorways of my mind, waiting for me to walk out. Mostly she still looks like she did as a young woman, wide-cheeked and prematurely wise. I am silent, as if I've swallowed my dreams, and words aren't sticking to the roof of my mouth.

She may be hoping for some big reveal. I too have questions about her own darn life. Suspicions of a partner who loved her like a runaway dog.

I've been better for a few years now—have been sitting on my life for a long time. I gaze at her face and remember what she looked like when we first met. And I remember how, even back then, I liked the faded parts of her best.

Mottled

The old girl and I: mottled, with stories of our impossible lives to share. How to begin?

Early days, drinking wine, watching the sun slide down behind the surrounding hills.

"I don't need to see palm trees," she said.

"Nor I," I said, rubbing an arthritic knee. Happy to remember them with her.

She stood in the kitchen as if leaning into the evening, staring at the tangled leaves of my spider plants.

"They've turned into the same plant," I said.

Dandy Indeed

"Taste is the first thing to go," she says, sipping water like a bird,
her eyeglass frames shining in the living room light.

We talk about our dandy curtains.
We roast pumpkin seeds just to smell them.

We race each other into the kitchen for blueberry pancakes,
thinking about what kind of syrup to warm.

Above Sadness

She says the neighbors notice everything we do.

She says, "let's bum them out."

I feel my faded freckles brighten.

"Dangerous," I say, wondering why I feel radical with unstable knees.

We have no idea what we're laughing about, and while she dips her spoon into her yogurt, I close my eyes. Later, I analyze her as she reads the paper, her long sad face when she lingers over the news. I urge her away from the window and into the kitchen where we can reset.

In my fluid dreams, the two of us barrel down the highway in a rain-splotched station wagon, moths on the wing.

Grand Entrances

At the Japanese lantern festival, the old girl and I hip-bump in, psyched about whatever people think of us, two zaps of purple in the crazy shuffle, licking wasabi from our lips, ignoring our hair, unpedicured, unmanicured, candid with hard-earned frumpiness. "You are my badge of honor," she says, holding my fingers. "You are my lantern in the wind."

Rosy

Late August we adopt a cat. The house brightens up. We name her after the pinkish-red clouds hanging around like half-eaten cotton candy. Rosy is a kisser, jumping on my desk, sniffing my lips. Twirling around in the living room chasing her tail.

"Did you know that a scattering of wavelengths and blue light in the sky could be so lovely?" she says as the sky turns even more rosy than the night before.

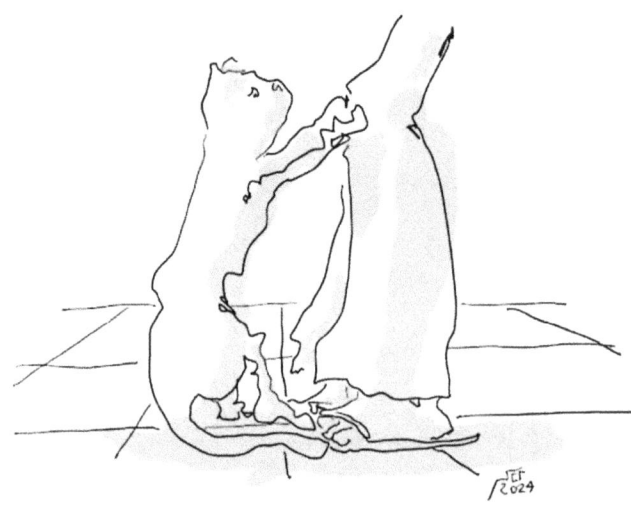

Snobby

The neighbors are snobby. They have better grass than we do, better quality dog poop from the bottoms of better-quality animals. Their sweaters lack unsightly balls. They stare at us from the safety of their perky living room patterns. Rosy would be unimpressive to them, sitting on the windowsill, bathing. We enjoy knowing that to them, our lives must seem as if they've been tossed randomly together. We're pleased with our sweatshirts and jeans, our re-loved sweaters rescued from the bidding wars of eBay.

No Nonsense

Self-appointed spinster she was—
I didn't
know it until then.
Those no-nonsense
cargo trousers,
practical handbag,
hair tied back
in a permanent tail—
I had to smile.
The turtle keychain
snapping from her pocket.
Crows chirping above her.

Frazzled, Fragile, Freckled

Now, all I wanted was to frolic and play with my companion. Freaky to have her back—freckled, frazzled. Still, I was fragile. I waddled around carefully, fretful over my frizzy hair, worried I'd fritter our time together away. Often, I found my body standing in a field, appeasing the clouds above me, fractal, built of never-ending patterns and pearly white freckles.

Thrillseekers

The boy who operates the Coaster looks as if he's going to be fired for letting two old thrill seekers on. His somber face takes in only small doses of understanding, poor child. So I'm thinking as the air whooshes out of my ears, and her gaping smile becomes an unlikely whiskey.

"I'm dying right next to you, Pet," she shrieks as we bounce and squawk and laugh, the cool bones of our ancient bottoms snapping against each other.

Beautiful Expanding Cat

Rosy the cat is watching us watch her. Sunny mornings just like this. We, proud of our cat. We, proud of our conversations. Nowhere else to be, nobody to impress, life in our tiny house. Her turtle keychain, my dumb hats. Moth-bitten sweaters, toothpaste splotched jeans. A beautiful, expanding cat.

Favorite Bench

"Didn't you ask me something important last night? Do you want to sit over there and talk about it?" she says.

When her cheeks broaden out, it's like the sun breaking through. She doesn't look like anyone else. "I didn't say that, exactly. I just wanted another slice of pizza."

She laughs and grabs my arm, leading me toward our favorite bench.

"We're spinsters. It doesn't take a whiz kid to see it," she says.

We toodle down the path, talking, happy because everything is as it should be. She has taken off her sun hat and is rubbing her neck.

"Don't you know? It's the opposite. It's always the opposite of what we thought it was going to be like when we were young."

Ancient Queens

We'd bop around the living room like college girls. We didn't care about our terrible skin. We woke up and laughed as we coned bitter coffee. Snickered about the neighbors and their overbred animals. We reminded our cat that her stomach was regal.

"Round kitties are the reincarnations of ancient queens," we said.

Invisibility

We stopped thinking about how much
or how little we worried anyone else.
There was sun in her hair and the sky was bruised,
like old movies that nobody else cared about.

Stepping Out

I sit with the cat
and remember
myself on the train,
smiling to myself in the window. *Hello,*
perky old you,
you with the green knit hat,
I would say to myself there.
The way it would feel to step onto a platform,
to mind all of the gaps.
And there was my friend
at the station to meet me,
to grin at my hat, not knowing
where we'd eat.
Where do you want to go? we'd both say.
Perfect,
not knowing.

Skating Rink

Near the end of Summer, we went to the ice-skating rink and I held her hand so we wouldn't fall. I was frightened of being without her. The demands of being alone had scared me to death.

"It's like this," I said, moving my feet, flushed from the goodness of gliding instead of limping.

Before and After

I went out into the night. It was windy and cold, and nobody else was stupidly standing out there. I thought about the men who had almost loved me, one after the other. I stood there thinking about how this was me before the old girl reemerged— a strange little alone person who walked outside at night for no reason other than studying the dark.

Now we sit on the sofa gawking at the snow on TV, Rosy nestled in the warm hollow between us. I raise my legs up and down with a therapy band. The snow piles up into a mountain of beauty. Looks so damn real, we think, forgetting it is.

Cat Proposal

It was the night you and the old girl propose to the cat. She has nothing left to prove to you. She is wild and pale and her eyes are green as pickles. You have stopped answering your phones, made changes to your wills.

"Rosy, will you?" the two of you chirp.

Just the sound of her name is a wedding gown.

Bountiful Chins

Today, I can see the crazy-assed fullness in both of our bountiful chins. "Your pancakes have done it," she clucks. There is pleasure in becoming as round as a cat. In the heat of the day, hanging around thinking about dinner. For exercise, slow walks on trails and talking too much while remembering to breathe.

"Do you have any memories of your father?" she asks. I try and conjure him, just for her: the time I stole a chocolate bar and got caught, how for once he didn't get mad as long as I gave him my half.

"That's funny," she says, our talks circling, our walks looking at pleasureful trees.

"Maybe it is," I reply.

We've given up everything. We're thriving.

Language

Sometimes when the old girl is snoring, I'm thrashing around thinking about how to snap a photo of the neighborhood fox. And tonight, even though it's freezing, we are walking along the dark trail, hoping to spot him. The moon is a flashing us like an exhibitionist. Tonight we're going to be lucky she says, her breath making a nest in the air. We know that this fox is close by, it's like we can smell him. Because of the moon, the old girl's hair glows like a tail.

City tour

That tour I took—remember?—of our hometown. I sat at the top of a double decker bus and, for a few seconds, it all felt familiar. Remember the snapshot, me the tourist? I had that smug-looking guy from Milwaukee take it. You can tell I felt like someone no longer really living there. I looked around as a visitor, the view like a secret.

Black Hole

You wake from a dream of her moving away like it's already happened, missing her Jupiter slippers, wrinkly smile. Wouldn't you spend your time better pulling her hair from the drain than wondering why you can't migrate to a climate without her?

No smile this morning, she's nibbled it down. But you walk into the kitchen anyway, like a hound sniffing for loss in the coffee, asking her how she'd like her eggs.

"I'm a slug," she says, getting up to leave. "Not going to fritter away the whole day."

By midday you'd spot her, sitting there in the sun like a Teflon pan, surface mildly scratched. So perfectly sunny in her sleeveless shirt, so easy to lose.

Dream of the Improved Town We Don't Belong In

In my dream we return to the place we grew up. Young women looked effervescent, sinewy, as we plant our feet a safe distance away in Birkenstocks.

"It's about endurance," I say. "And hammertoes," she sighs, looking down at her curled up babies. Plunking down on the pavement in front of the swanky bar where the glittery girls are pooling.

"Not here," I tsk.

"Then where?" she replies, fearless, nearly arrested last week floating up lower State Street, feathers from our pillows falling like entrails.

Retired Acrobat

She saw herself as a retired acrobat
rising from her chair and gliding
wearing the exact blue of her younger eyes.

She was dancing, flying, jumping
into the sea from a cliff. Rising
from the sadness, smooth
as a worry stone.

A performer, fallen
from men's trapezes,
always just missing the safety net.

Plunking Away on the Sofa

It trickles down from my scalp as if it doesn't know where to go or how to stop going there. "Stop moping about your mop," the old girl says. She smiles at me as if I'm perfectly imperfect and sits with the rosy cat while I plunk away on my ukulele, singing "When the Saints Come Marching In" to an audience of whiskers.

"All we need now is a New Orleans funeral," she laughs, her arms around the cat—the three of us floating away to the islands.

Swallowed Hope

The day you started to think about how dreams dissolve: it begins in the throat, when you refuse to say anything about what really matters. You remembered the story your friend told you about the singer who lost her voice.

"Did she get it back?" you asked.

"No," she said. "Because nothing else needed to be sung."

Collector of Days

Late August, the dampness eased. We watched a squirrel collect nuts and take them back to her nest. I told the old girl, It's almost September, you're still here. She smiled. Where else? At the pond in the woods, we cast our fingers into the water, felt the cold sting. At the end of each dripping day we swung on the porch, kissing the rims of our wine glasses.

Becoming Unpeeled

"My palms are orange," I said, and she laughed. She too had been eating too many carrots, thought we might be overdoing them. I stared at my hands.

"Today I feel like a horse," I said. Things could go on like this, till one or both of us died. The fridge bloomed orange.

"Peeled or raw?" she asked. She brought me a rough, original carrot, naked on a plate.

Chill

Midnight, I sense the old girl floating around the living room as if a ghost lives inside her. I get out of bed, ask her what's the matter.

There is a halo around Rosy's head.

"I miss her already even though she's young," she says.

"It's a good idea to befriend another creature," I say.

There's always a chill in the house before we meet up in the warm kitchen.

Old Photo

There you were humming them songs. There you were feeling fat inside your clothes even though you were trim. There you were in the midst of your one-time-only beauty, a beauty you'd rent for a decade and then decide it had been enough.

There you were in your mother's house, the one she loved because it was her own and she could tear down walls and build cupboards, the one she'd have to sell when she got cancer.

There you were baking cookies for the relatives, listening to Lovely Rita—already sad about how temporary it was.

You, as a sexy meter maid.

Stride

"Enough with this Disneyland shit," a neighbor yells at another neighbor, because a gathering of garden gnomes have taken over their front yard. One of them standing on its head. They are silly, and yet it doesn't bother us. We stare out the window, wondering if the thistles in our garden are ever going to bloom again. There are holes in her jeans, a few wine stains on mine. One of the stains is the shape of an elongated animal. That might be our fox, right there, she says. We close the curtains and pour a few early glasses of wine. The neighbor continues to huff and puff, as if wishing to blow the other neighbor's house down.

Crispy

She was addicted to her electric blanket,
but no longer trusted it: that article
about the lonely woman
who'd overused a blanket to cheer herself up
and accidentally roasted herself in her sleep.

There may as well have been crispy
potatoes as a side.

Hips and Wings

When I was fourteen, my hips were like the wings of a wild, uncomfortable bird. My friend's? Agile. When we rode bikes together, her wings followed me out of the craziest places, away from her nosy parents, from my mother who never trusted her own winged breadth. Together our lives could improve, we could find an alley to live in as pigeons. Could fly on bikes, think about how little it all mattered. I wanted to blend, live in a narrow house, cultivate skinny dreams. Wanted to survive on water and air and melba toast. So happy next to each other, wobbling like palm trees.

Rangy Boyfriend

We've fallen under the spell of a fox. First, we spy it limping away from the garbage can, pizza crust lodged in its mouth. He's like a rangy boyfriend. We splash our faces with water. How drab life would be without his visits! Because of him, there's no evidence of our pizza indulgence. Kissing these summer days goodbye, we lean into our take-out menus, planning for the red-eared ruffian.

Metronome

Night passed, and we breakfasted in the dark, listening. Eating pancakes. Talking animatedly about nothing. Remembering.

The sun came up too soon.

"I wish I could still trust these knees," I say, looking down.

"And I," she said, chewing on the good side of her mouth, clacking like a metronome.

Memory of Being a Seed

I explained to the old girl how it started:

The first man I was in love with said he was going to keep me—maybe, if his parents approved. Waiting was part of the deal. He said that we were like a seed, that we needed to water ourselves, then sit back and see, while they stuffed him full of solutions for the practical gardener. "They're just a bit unsure if we'll flourish, planted right next to each other," he said. "Just kiss me," I thought, like a piece of stolen fruit.

What is Felt

We walk to the bakery.
We sit in the living room eating.
We look at the crumbs on our socks.
We forgive ourselves for the mess.

Night comes on, and out pops the hidden fox.
We call Rosy to make sure she's safe.

I start with *That day the hermit woke up*
with a bubble in his heart.
She says
And then he realized he could still feel
so what did it matter?

Salty

Later that morning, my cheeks became salty, but not as salty as the Pacific ocean, where we would always have younger memories of time together; not as salty as my skin when I told her how I remembered; not as salty as our early days of rain in a car with no functional windshield wipers, when our stars became all mixed up.

On A Winter's Night, No Traveler

On a cold winter night she was thinking about the kind of house they might move into together after the winter ended, when they got out from the mud. She was tired of missing a warm sweater that would have made the long season easier. There was a stain on the rug from red wine which had slopped from the counter during what must have been an earthquake last summer, although she never heard anything in the news about it. The stain reminded her of a purple orchid, the kind that died if you watered it or that died if you didn't water it. She couldn't remember. In her questionable life with exotic flowers, orchids always died, no matter what. How much she loved them, how many ways she talked to them. Flowers that bloomed in darkness, as she wanted to bloom for someone else.

A Fly Can Ruin Her Act

The tight rope was strung in the living room, and the old girl was walking it again, hoping that after her performance she would land in the same place on the sofa. She looked young, a woman with gravity on her side. "You're almost back," I said, as she tried not to smile too heavily to either side.

Old Girls Glow

Inside the living room candles finally flickered off, I could see all of the marks, and now there was only a large, sweet cat next to the empty popcorn tub on the sofa, and a Christmas morning vision that ours was not a beauty of a house, but a rectangular rental bungalow that we both really liked. These were the thoughts I was having, a blanket wrapped around my frozen shoulder.

Backwards Remembering

4. When we got tired of talking about the futility of rootedness, she asked me to change the channel. The discussion was annoying her. Her tiny silver earrings glittered like mercury balls.

3. "I'm too much of an asshole for marriage," she once boasted, when we were playing in the waves, the frothy kind that nobody but us waded in.

2. Sometimes she resembled a hedgehog stuck in a paper bag, so I hugged her and said I was off to pick up some croissants, something to cheer us up before another week of rain.

1. The palm-tree-shaped stain on the wall was not getting smaller. In fact it wasn't shaped like a tree at all.

Vision of a Nicer You

Today I walked past myself on a bench at the sharp corner of St. Anne's Garden. I checked me out—an old girl with a very old smile—thought that I had once been pretty. A rich, handsome boyfriend might even have made me a cheese and tomato panini for lunch.

"Do you hurt people?" I asked myself and responded that yes, I was not the person I had always wanted to be.

The curly cartoon clouds, nonchalant, poked each other.

Non-Veterinarian Surprise

He's early. The doorbell gooses us. Calming ourselves, we open the door for an on-call veterinarian we've never seen before. "Come in."

On the sofa, blind, demented Rosie is dreaming up butterflies, her skinny bones poking through fur.

The vet half-smiles, looking around the living room.

"She has no interest in eating, doesn't know who we are anymore, gets lost at the end of the hallway."

He stares at us, looking from one to the other.

"If this was your cat, what would you do?"

"Do?" he says. "I'm here to pick up the give-away chair from Buy and Sell."

We laugh.

Asleep between us, our Rosie is dreaming, envisioning critters she used to be able to see.

Salamanders

Rain falls all summer, and the salamanders—dark, sad—find their way into the garage. They resemble sleepy old grandfathers, their heavy-lidded eyes buggy and plump. Each day we lift another into the top of an empty pizza carton to transport it back to the garden. *We love this country too*, we say, *but you don't want to die out here alone.*

What Happened While Nobody Was Watching

2.

Her young self died. With nothing left to do, she decided. When she had nothing left to work on, nobody to worry about, she shrank into a puff of smoke, swirled for a last look around the living room (hoping for a comfortable place to sit, all of her chairs sucked) and then she was gone.

1.

She woke up old, she woke up better. She had nothing to do now, and she was glad. She had nothing to do, and she was tired. This made it easier. She was done.

3.

She turned on the television and stared at the movie channel. There was nothing she wanted to see. She had seen it all before.

Sometimes she remembered her mother's tired eyes.

She decided that life was a lost movie, one that was never released because the budget died.

4.

She remembered that she used to want a pet fox.

She remembered her young, boisterous glow.

Before the Old Girl Did (or Didn't) Arrive

She's patting a fuzzy fleece pillow, imagining the warm belly of her childhood dog. Before that, she's marveling at the humid living room, thinking that she should open the windows before they stick. Before that she's craving a gooey pizza, sharing it with a friend. Before that, she rises from the daydream in which a creature with wild, unruly hair wakes her with kisses. What kind of lover is this? she laughs. Before that, it's morning and she's removing bits of crust from the corners of her eyes.

I'm in it for the long haul, she tells herself, standing from the bed, floating through the quiet house.

Impermanence

Most days I worry. My hair's falling out all over the living room sofa. "Hair loss means stress," an advice column says. "It's damaging to think too much."

My brother calls to let me know that he's had a heart attack. "Just a mini," he says, "nothing interesting."

I never know what to believe when it comes to my family, a roomful of unreliable characters.

And there is the broken clock, ghosts of dead relatives.

I find a bottle of old perfume, smelling like a love letter I forgot to answer.

Gliding and Groaning

At the skating rink I wobbled with unforgiving knees but didn't fall this time, paddling the air with my hands. "This is the first time I have skated in fifty years," I said to the worried people gliding past me.

'Poor old lunatic' they probably thought.

But I really just wanted to do this for her, and so I moved myself awkwardly toward a woman who reminded me of my old dear friend, a woman with a South Sea smile but no parrot.

A woman with flailing but open arms.

My legs splayed apart from each other like friends floating in different directions, but I forced them back together, heading for the wall.

At Home in the Dream

We were playing parts we could barely remember. I was playing the chameleon. She was the sage. We walked outside, having the times of our lives. We looked up at the sky, dark as an old bruise. Her eyes were full of dreams, her hair full of sun. Then she turned, too quickly, and I woke up.

Why did I always arise so early? What was the point of setting an alarm? A long day ahead. "I'm back," I said. "Rats."

British Palm Trees

Did she laugh or the phone hiccough? I remember her child-wide cheeks—picture them rising over a new continent, a helium balloon bringing me home to my past.

I don't care if you ever actually get here, I repeat in a warm, low voice, as if I'm finally being heard. I don't say that I am crying.

I am dreaming about how good it will be to see her old; how, together, we can hunt for British palm trees. I remember those trees always standing around and leaning a bit forward, ready for anything—willing to catch me.

About the Author

MEG POKRASS is the award-winning author of 8 flash fiction collections and 2 flash novellas, including *Spinning to Mars* (Blue Light Book Award, 2021) and *The Loss Detector* (Bamboo Dart Press, 2020). Her work has appeared in over 900 literary journals has been anthologized in 3 Norton anthologies: *Flash Fiction International* (W.W. Norton, 2015), *New Micro: Exceptionally Short Fiction* (W.W. Norton, 2018), and *Flash Fiction America* (W. W. Norton & Co., 2023). She is the Series Co-Editor of *Best Microfiction* and Founding Editor of *New Flash Fiction Review*. Meg lives in Inverness Scotland.

http://www.megpokrass.com

112 N. Harvard Ave. #65
Claremont, CA 91711

chapbooks@bamboodartpress.com

www.bamboodartpress.com

www.ingramcontent.com/pod-product-compliance
Lightning Source LLC
Chambersburg PA
CBHW081145170626
46809CB00011B/3162